Saturday Popular Concerts.

DIRECTOR—Mr. S. ARTHUR CHAPPELL.

Four Hundred and Ninety-seventh Concert.

PROGRAMME FROM THE WORKS OF

Various Masters.

SATURDAY AFTERNOON, DECEMBER 19th, 1874.

OCTETT, for two Violins, Viola, Violoncello, Double Bass.
Clarionet, French Horn, and Bassoon. *Schubert.*

(Twelfth performance at the Popular Concerts.)

Adagio, leading to Allegro—F major.
Andante un poco mosso—B flat major.
Scherzo, allegro vivace—F major; with Trio—C major.
Andante with variations—C major.
Minuetto—F major; with Trio—B flat major.
Andante molto; leading to
Finale, allegro—F major.

Herr STRAUS, Herr L. RIES, Mr. ZERBINI,
Mr. LAZARUS, M. PAQUIS, Mr. WINTERBOTTOM,
Mr. REYNOLDS, and Signor PIATTI.

This remarkable piece is one of the very many works
which were not published till after Schubert's death. During
life his creative activity was ceaseless, and work upon
work in every form of composition came with astonishing

Twelfth Concert of the Seventeenth Season.

rapidity from his pen. With true Shakesperian carelessness about present fame, he published few or none of the most important of these pieces. He wrote because he could not help it, and left the offspring of his brain to find their way into the world's appreciation as best they might, apparently unconcerned as to their future destiny, whether they were to be heard and appreciated by thousands of enthusiastic amateurs, or end in being disposed of as mere waste paper! Since Schubert's death, however, Mendelssohn, who loved everything that had a touch of genius in it, and could not be insensible to the romantic beauty of many of Schubert's compositions, took up the cause of his instrumental music (the songs had earlier been understood and admired by every one with any pretensions to musical sensibility), and, by his powerful influence at Leipsic and elsewhere, created a general desire among all musicians and patrons of music to know them. Robert Schumann, too, did much towards the same end by his eloquent writings and criticisms ; and now that both Mendelssohn and Schumann have gone to join their much-loved brother in art, Schubert's reputation has so enormously increased, that the likelihood is rather of his being over-estimated than not thought enough of.

The Octett is calculated to increase the almost universal interest now felt in the instrumental music of its gifted composer. A reference to the principal themes of each of its movements is subjoined :—

Introductory Adagio.

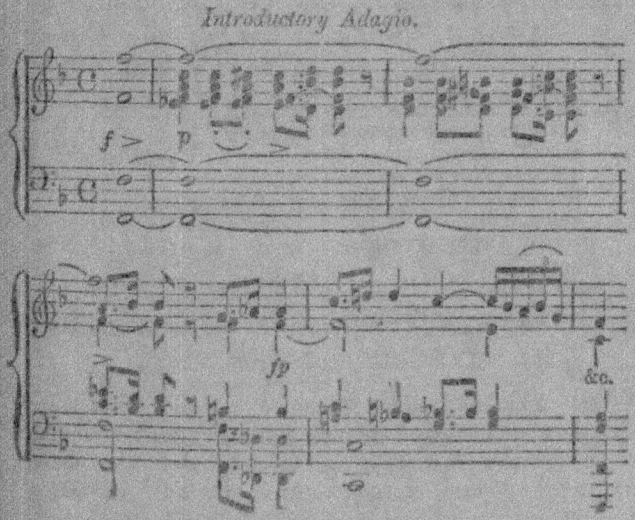

Allegro (first theme).

(Second Subject—D minor and F major.)

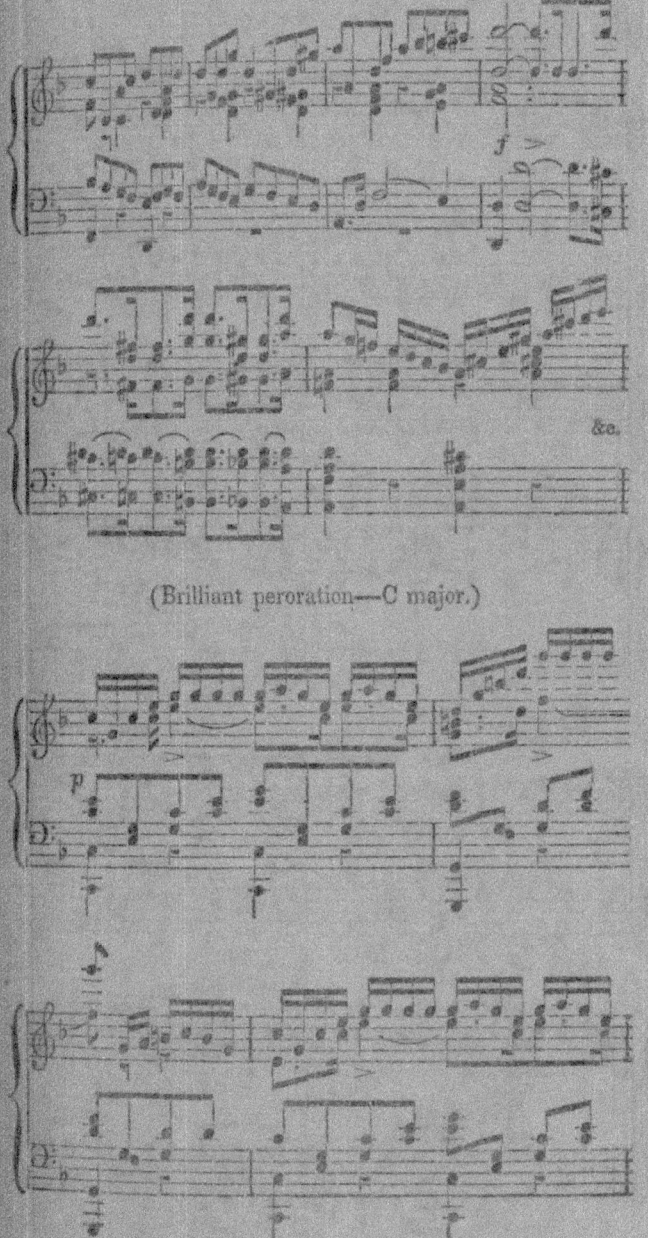

(Brilliant peroration—C major.)

Andante.

un poco mosso.

Scherzo.

Trio (C major).

The next two movements (*andante* with variations, in C major, and *minuetto* with *trio*, in F and B flat) are omitted. These movements are strongly impregnated with the spirit of Spohr, both in melody and harmony—a rare phenomenon in Schubert.

Andante (introductory to finale).

Finale (first theme).

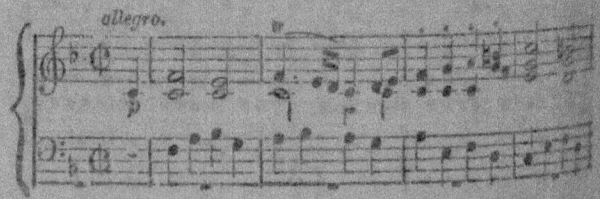

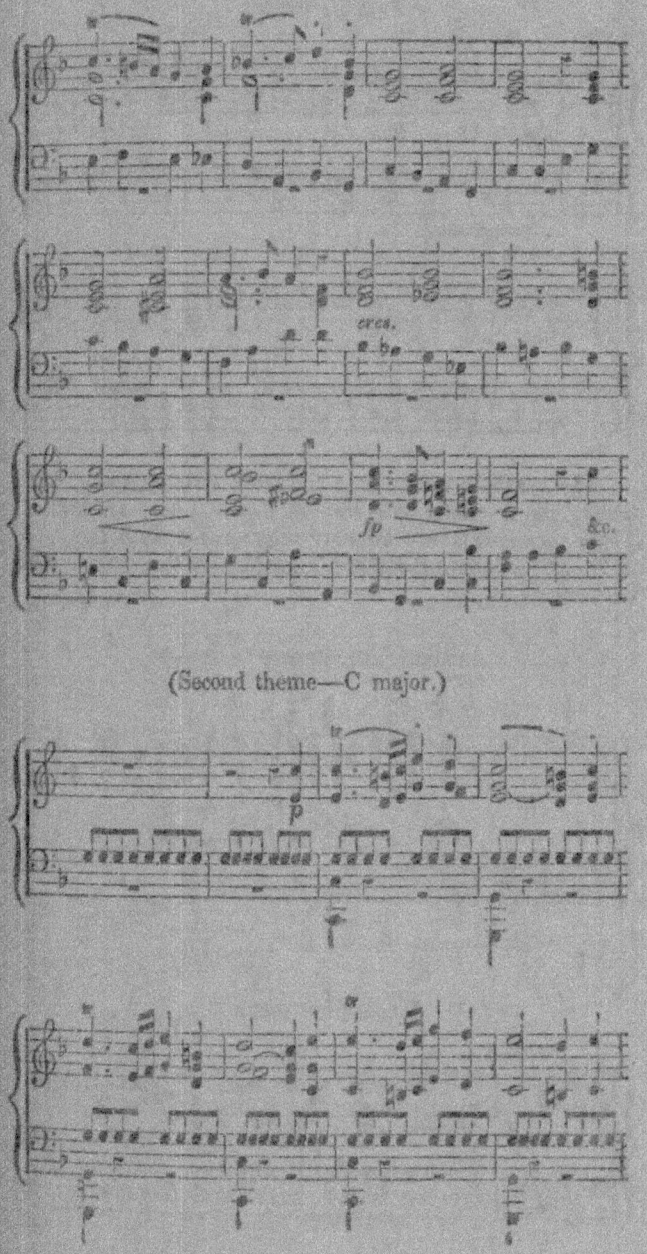

(Second theme—C major.)

The Octett of Schubert was composed at Vienna, in 1824 (four years before the death of its composer), for Count Ferdinand Troyer. The autograph is in the possession of Herr Spina, to whom the indication, "Opus 116" is attributable.

Franz Schubert was born on the 31st of January, 1797, in one of the suburbs of Vienna, where his father lived as a schoolmaster. At the age of seven years he received his first instruction in music from Michael Holzer, cantor in the parish church of the neighbouring village. Holzer recognised the fine gifts of the boy, and procured his admission into the Imperial school. Schubert was then (1808) eleven years old, and received at once the title of court singer. He afterwards became solo singer in the Imperial chapel, and took lessons on the piano and violin. His progress was so rapid that, at the orchestra rehearsals, where he played first violin, he used to conduct in the absence of the director. The Imperial Court Organist, Ruzicka, gave him lessons in thorough bass, and subsequently the Imperial Kapellmeister, the famous Salieri, instructed him in composition. Finally, he owed, as he himself confessed, the completion of his musical education to the best and most admired master-works of Mozart, Haydn, and Beethoven. Yet Schubert never gave up his own habits of severe study, and even in the last months of his life applied himself diligently to counterpoint under the direction of his friend, the Court Organist, Simon Sechter. After he had spent five years in the Imperial School, Schubert's voice broke, and as his yearning for musical knowledge grew more and more urgent, he left this preparatory school in the year 1813, and devoted himself entirely to composition. From that time he lived in the paternal house, and afterwards alone, supporting himself by giving lessons and by the sale of his works. With the exception of a few excursions to Hungary, Styria, and Upper Austria, Schubert remained constantly at Vienna, partly in the city itself, partly in the country, where the healthiest influences inspired his fruitful genius. His life was no way eventful, and so he could devote himself in perfect quiet to his art. Unhappily, and, alas! too early, his labours were for ever interrupted. A fever snatched him from the world on the 19th of November, 1828, in his thirty-second year. His death was felt most painfully, not only by his friends, but by every one in Germany who took an interest in music. A great number of artists and lovers of art accompanied him to the last resting place, and solemn masses for the dead were performed in his honour at Vienna and other large cities.

RECIT. ED ARIA, Miss LEONORA BRAHAM.

(*L'Amor Vendicato.*)   Paesiello.

RECIT.

Crudele! or coldi piangi,
Che spingesti tu stesso
A si tragico fin? Misera Dafne!
Ma più misero Alceo! Tutto perdesti,
    Che ti resta a sperar? Così il destino,
Aminta ingannator, cangiò d'aspetto! ahi lasso!
Questo e il piacer, questo il contento? Apollo,
Che ad Alceo promettesti? Amore! Apollo!
Numi tutti del Ciel; che in tronco, in sasso,
In erme alpestra rupe
Per pietà mi trasforma! e tu, sollievo
D'un disperato cor, perchè non vieni
Morte, il corso a troncar de' mali miei?
Ahi! meco sol tanto crudel, tu sei!

ARIA.

Ho perduto il bel semblante,
Nè non trovo alcun ristoro;
Ho perduto il mio tesoro,
La mia Ninfa, oh dio, dov'è?
Questi monti, e queste piante
Sempre udranno i miei lamenti,
Chi mai vide tra viventi;
Sventurato al par di me?

Dafne mia, felice amante,
Vissi ognor a te d'appresso:
Odio or tutto, odio me stesso
Che diviso io son da te.

Giovanni Paesiello (or Paisiello), was not only a great musician, but was possessed of a large fund of information, conversant with the dead languages, well-read in all branches of literature, and on terms of friendship with the most distinguished persons of the age. He composed seventy-eight operas—twenty-seven serious and fifty-one comic,—eight "intermezzos," and many cantatas, oratorios, masses, and motettos, "*Te Deums*," symphonies, pianoforte pieces, &c. &c. He died at Naples, June 5th, 1816, aged 76.

SONATA, in C sharp minor, Op. 27, No. 1, "The Moonlight," for Pianoforte aione.* *Beethoven.*

(By desire.)

(Twelfth performance at the Popular Concerts.)

Adagio—C sharp minor.
Allegretto—D flat major.
Presto agitato—C sharp minor.

Dr. HANS VON BÜLOW.

The origin of the name "Moonlight-Sonata" (*Mond-scheins-Sonate*), so generally given to the Sonata in C sharp minor, is attributed to the late Herr Rellstab, who, in one of his critical essays, compares it to "a barque visiting by moonlight the wild coasts of the lake of the four Cantons." There was a story at Vienna, that Beethoven improvised the *adagio* in the garden of the Countess Guicciardi, of whom at one time he was a devoted admirer, and to whom, four years later, he addressed the three passionate letters, dated from Hungary, which his biographer Schindler has given to the world.

The original title of the Sonata was "*Sonate quasi una Fantasia dedicata alla Damigalla Contessa Giulietta Guicciardi.*" In Germany it is occasionally recognised as the "*Lauben Sonate.*" Next, perhaps, to the one in A flat, Op. 26, and the *Sonate Pathetique*, Op. 13, the "Moonlight Sonate" is the most widely known and popular of all the works that Beethoven wrote for the pianoforte. It is one of those compositions in which he is completely himself, and which bear no trace of any extraneous influence. The *adagio* in C sharp minor, with which it opens, would alone be enough to distinguish it from all previous or subsequent models. Beethoven has indicated at the head of the first page the manner in which he conceives the movement should be played :—*Se deve suonare tutto questo pezzo delicatissimamente e senza sordino.*" The figure of accompaniment, in triplet-arpeggio, *sempre pianissimo e senza sordino*, which is never once arrested during the progress of the *adagio*, and the plaintive melody upon which the entire movement is constructed :—

* No. 18 of Beethoven's Sonatas, edited by Mr. CHARLES HALLE—Published by CHAPPELL and Co. 50, New Bond Street.

—gliding at once into the relative major of the key (E), makes this direction sufficiently intelligible. The development of this highly impressive *adagio* is marked by such a constant succession of beauties, that it is impossible to refer to more than a few of them. Subjoined is a point that will not escape observation :—

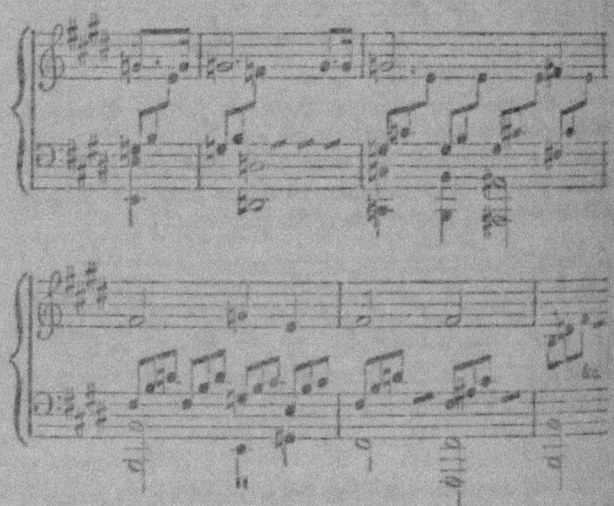

This delicate modulation is the introduction to what may be termed the second subject, which, commencing in B :—

—comes to a definite close in F sharp, the subdominant minor of the original key :—

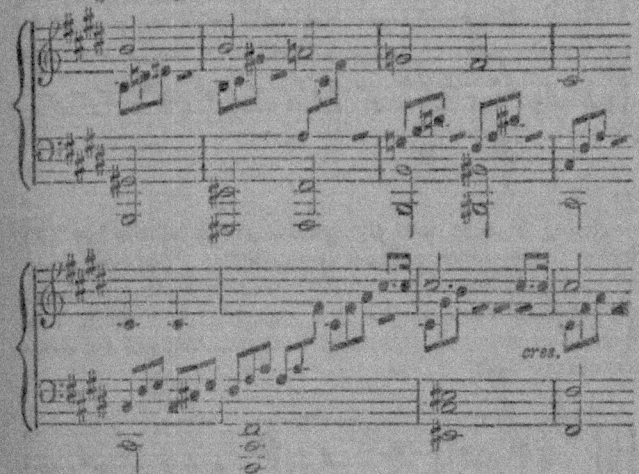

In this tone the principal theme is further developed, until, through another transition, no less natural and at the same time impressive, we come to a new melody in the dominant of the key (G sharp)—minor again, in keeping with the prevalent sombreness of the movement :—

This now occurs as the dominant pedal, which, by means of an appropriate passage, built upon its harmonies, diatonic and chromatic, brings us back once more, without the intervention of a "second part," to the first subject in C sharp minor :—

After the transition to E major (already noticed) is repeated, the resumption of the second subject, in the key of the *adagio* (C sharp), is prepared by the subjoined progression, in which the intensely impassioned effect of the D natural (an instance of Beethoven's always effective employment of the minor second of the scale) can hardly fail to arrest attention:—

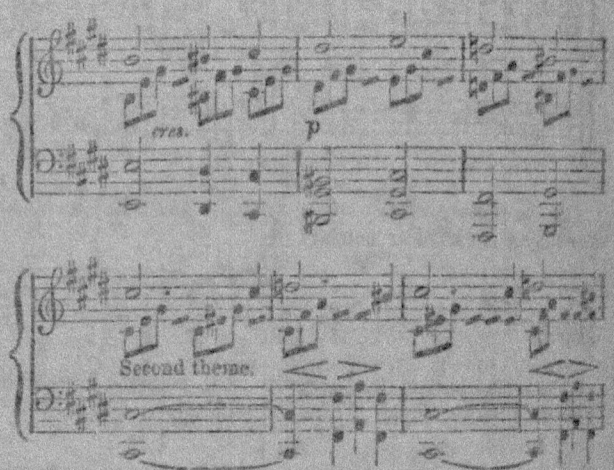

The last reference to the opening bars of the principal theme, or melody, is given, as a middle part, to the left hand:—

The reiteration of this one particular note (G) suggests the idea of prostration—as if the composer, unable to proceed, had left off in despair, just at the point where he began. No more perfect " Song without Words " exists than this beautiful slow movement.

The *allegretto* or *scherzo*—which, perhaps to simplify the signature and accommodate ordinary readers, Beethoven writes in D flat, rather than in C sharp, the real major of his first key—has been likened poetically, by a famous pianist,* to "a flower between two abysses" ("*une fleur entre deux abîmes*"). Certainly no more striking and grateful contrast to what precedes and follows, than its first innocent and cheerful theme, could be imagined :—

At the repeat, instead of being (like the bass) identical, this subject is varied as beneath :—

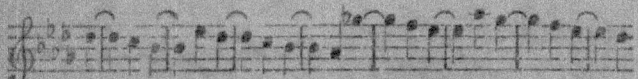

The second part of the *scherzo* is, if possible, even more beautiful than the first. Thus insinuatingly it sets out :—

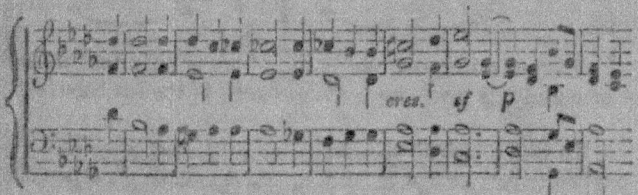

The theme of the *trio* is more pensive, but scarcely less melodious than that of its companion :—

* Liszt.

On the whole, it may be urged that the simile of the famous pianist is by no means so fantastic as such poetical comparisons frequently are.

The *presto agitato*—which, on account of its difficulty, has helped in some degree to restrict what would otherwise, in all likelihood, have been the *universal* popularity of the sonata in C sharp minor—sets out impetuously :—

The second section of the leading subject (like all that follows) is in keeping :—

In the principal second theme, the restless semiquaver motion which, except in one instance, is kept up incessantly to the end of the movement, is now allotted to the left hand—as accompaniment to a melody, the agitated character of which is in strict sympathy with the context :—

The natural development of this new subject—which appears, as will be observed, in the minor dominant of the first key—is suddenly arrested by a bold transition into A major, once more showing Beethoven's happy invention in the employment of the minor second of the key as an exhaustless source of contrast and variety :—

The relief afforded to the elsewhere almost unceasing prevalence of the minor key by this transition, though brief and evanescent, is most grateful. The three bars of A major are twice introduced, precisely in the same manner, and twice in the same manner relapse to G sharp minor—as if they had got loose by accident, and were suddenly arrested in their unexpected course of freedom. A new and very impassioned episode is now presented, remarkable as the solitary instance alluded to of the semiquaver-motion being for a time suspended :—

When this has been brought to its full close, it gives way to another episode, and the return of the semiquaver figure of accompaniment. This new feature may be recognised by the melody alone:—

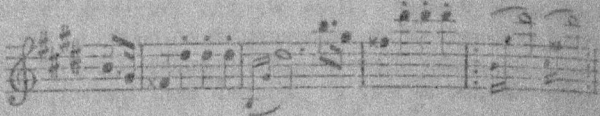

With the foregoing the first part of the *presto agitato* is brought to a conclusion, in the same energetic style that characterises it at the outset. The second part is chiefly formed upon the first and second leading themes. Among other striking points, a very fine modulation, from F sharp minor (in which key the second subject first makes its appearance) into G major, is noticeable, both for its own sake and as a new example of the repose afforded by a transitory reference to the major key:—

In the course of the development of the foregoing, the principal subject is resumed, by means of a somewhat lengthy episode, constructed upon the dominant pedal bass (G sharp), and formed out of the melody subjoined:—

The first part is then resumed *notatim*, until the appearance of the second subject proper, in C sharp minor. This is again arrested by a transition to the major (now of D), and proceeds exactly in the same manner as before, allowing for the difference of keys, until quite a new passage, in diminished sevenths, abruptly suspends the climax, and ushers in the never-failing "coda." Here we find no change in the passionate character of the movement, which, on the contrary, assumes still greater intensity in its treatment of one of the leading melodies, as may be gathered from the subjoined extract :—

A brilliant passage of arpeggios (resembling the improvised "cadence" introduced by a ready player into a concerto), followed by a chromatic ascending scale, now leads to a pause and "*point d'orgue :*"

The "*tempo primo*" is then resumed; and after a brief allusion to one of the melodies already quoted—

—the movement ends, in the impetuous and passionate style that characterises it throughout.

The second of the two sonatas, Op. 27, was advertised by the publisher, Cappi, in the *Wiener Zeitung* of March 3, 1809, as "*ganz neu erschienen.*"

The Sonata in C sharp minor was first introduced by Herr Lubeck, at the twenty-second concert of the second second—May 21, 1860.

. Dr. HANS VON BÜLOW will perform on one of Messrs. JOHN BROADWOOD and SONS' Concert Grand Pianofortes.

SONG, Miss LEONORA BRAHAM. *Schubert.*

"MEINE RUH' IST HIN."

Meine Ruh' ist hin, mein Herz ist schwer,
Ich finde sie nimmer und nimmer mehr!
Wo ich ihn nicht hab' ist mir das Grab,
Die ganze Welt ist mir vergällt,
Mein armer Kopf ist mir verrückt,
Mein armer Sinn ist mir zerstückt.

Nach ihm nur schau' ich zum Fenster hinaus,
Nach ihm nur geh' ich aus dem Haus.
Sein hoher Gang, sein ed'le Gestalt,
Seines Mundes Lächeln, seiner Augen Gewalt,
Und seiner Rede Zauberfluss,
Sein Händedruck, und ach, sein Kuss!

Mein Busen drängt sich nach ihm hin,
Ach dürft' ich fassen und halten ihn,
Und küssen ihn, so wie ich wollt',
An seinen Küssen vergehen sollt'.
O könnt' ich ihn küssen, so wie ich wollt',
An seinen Küssen vergehen sollt'.

The song of Margaret at the spinning-wheel ("Gretchen am Spinnrade,") in Goethe's *Faust,* was published by Diabelli in 1821, as Schubert's Op. 2—Op. 1 being the "Erl King." The autograph is in the Royal Library at Berlin.

———

SONATA, in B flat major, Op. 45, for Pianoforte
and Violoncello. *Mendelssohn.*

(Fifth performance at the Popular Concerts.)

Allegro vivace—B flat major.
Andante—G minor.
Allegro assai—B flat major.

Dr. HANS VON BÜLOW and Signor PIATTI.

Mendelssohn composed two sonatas for pianoforte and
violoncello, of which the one introduced this evening is the
first. Like its companion (in D), the sonata in B flat is
constructed on the regular form which Haydn and Mozart
brought to perfection, and of which the exploring mind of
Beethoven only enlarged the scope and dimensions. The
opening theme of the *allegro vivace* might have proceeded
from Mozart himself:—

The second subject, however, is peculiar to Mendelssohn:—

—and, in the progress of its development, remarkable for the manner in which a full close, in the key of the dominant (F), to which it should properly belong, is every where ingeniously avoided.

The theme of the *andante*—one of the loveliest and most touching Mendelssohn ever invented—could hardly be mistaken for the inspiration of any other composer:—

Andante.

The whole of this movement—temporarily relieved by a short and tuneful episode in the major key of G:—

Violoncello.

— is carried on in the same quaint and plaintive style. It is one of its author's most highly finished and characteristic pieces.

The *finale*—in the *rondo* form—is built upon the subjoined fresh, expressive, and spontaneous melody:—

This movement is quite as interesting and quite as admirable as its two companions, and by its unaffected style and catching tunefulness is likely to make an impression as quickly and as emphatically as the *andante* itself.

The Sonata in B flat major was first introduced by Mr. Charles Hallé and Signor Piatti, at the eleventh concert of the fifth season—January 12th, 1863.

END OF THE FOUR HUNDRED AND NINETY-SEVENTH CONCERT.

J. MALLETT, PRINTER, 59, WARDOUR STREET, SOHO.

MONDAY POPULAR CONCERTS.

MONDAY EVENING, JANUARY 11th, 1875.

PROGRAMME.

PART I.

QUINTET, in A major, for two Violins, two Violas, and
Violoncello..*Mendelssohn.*

MM. STRAUS, L. RIES, ZERBINI, BURNETT, and PIATTI.

NEW SONG, "Tender and true."..*Sullivan.*

Miss EDITH WYNNE.

PRELUDE and FUGUE à la Tarentella, for Pianoforte
alone ....*Bach.*

Madlle. MARIE KREBS.

PART II.

TRIO, in B flat, Op. 97, for Pianoforte, Violin, and
Violoncello..*Beethoven.*

Madlle. MARIE KREBS, MM. STRAUS and PIATTI.

SONG, "Versar nel mio cor."..*Gounod.*

Miss EDITH WYNNE.

FANTASIA, in C major, Op. 159, for Pianoforte and
Violin ....*Schubert.*

Madlle. MARIE KREBS and Herr STRAUS.

Conductor - - Mr. ZERBINI.

www.ingramcontent.com/pod-product-compliance
Lightning Source LLC
Chambersburg PA
CBHW082053220626
47052CB00006B/1225